JAN KARON

Jeremy
The Tale of
an Honest Bunny

illustrated by Teri Weidner

PUFFIN BOOKS
An Imprint of Penguin Group (USA) Inc.

Puffin Books
Published by the Penguin Group
Penguin Young Readers Group, 345 Hudson Street, New York, New York 10014, U.S.A.
Penguin Group (Canada), 90 Eglinton Avenue East, Suite 700, Toronto, Ontario, Canada M4P 2Y3
(a division of Pearson Penguin Canada Inc.)
Penguin Books Ltd, 80 Strand, London WC2R 0RL, England
Penguin Ireland, 25 St Stephen's Green, Dublin 2, Ireland (a division of Penguin Books Ltd)
Penguin Group (Australia), 250 Camberwell Road, Camberwell, Victoria 3124, Australia
(a division of Pearson Australia Group Pty Ltd)
Penguin Books India Pvt Ltd, 11 Community Centre, Panchsheel Park, New Delhi – 110 017, India
Penguin Group (NZ), 67 Apollo Drive, Rosedale, Auckland 0632, New Zealand
(a division of Pearson New Zealand Ltd.)
Penguin Books (South Africa) (Pty) Ltd, 24 Sturdee Avenue,
Rosebank, Johannesburg 2196, South Africa

Penguin Books Ltd, Registered Offices: 80 Strand, London WC2R 0RL, England

First published in the United States of America by Viking,
a division of Penguin Putnam Books for Young Readers, 2000
Published by Puffin Books, a member of Penguin Young Readers Group, 2013

1 3 5 7 9 10 8 6 4 2

Text copyright © Jan Karon, 2000
Illustrations copyright © Teri Weidner, 2000
All rights reserved

THE LIBRARY OF CONGRESS HAS CATALOGED THE VIKING EDITION AS FOLLOWS:
Karon, Jan, date-.
Jeremy: the tale of an honest bunny / by Jan Karon ; illustrated by Teri Weidner.
p.   cm.
Summary: Unwilling to be sent to America in a box, Jeremy, a very special rabbit,
sets off to make his own way to his new home, with his maker's blessing to
keep him safe through a series of adventures.
ISBN 0-670-88104-X
[1. Rabbits—Fiction. 2. Toys—Fiction. 3. Voyages and travel—Ficiton.
4. Christian life—Fiction.] I. Weidner, Teri, ill.
II. Title.
PZ7.K146Je   [E]—dc21   2000   98-53757   CIP   AC

Puffin Books 978-0-14-242537-4

Manufactured in China
Set in Bembo

A made-up story for my daughter, Candace.

May her own journey bring her safely Home.

A Vest with Silver Buttons

*E*very summer evening in the softly gathering dusk, John Sweeney appeared on the path that led through the high sheep meadow.

To his mind, the sheep had taken to greeting him. And after his walk from the village, a bit of conversation was welcome.

"Baaa-aa-aa!" they cried.

"Hello yourself!" he sang out.

On either side of the winding lane to his cottage, tall hedgerows brimmed with wild roses and white-flowering bindweed. And deep in the tangle of the thick hedge, creatures were settling down contentedly, just as he would soon do himself.

As he rounded the bend where the hawthorn grew, he saw his own small cottage standing in the midst of a garden drenched with evening birdsong.

Without knowing it, he took his cap from his head and held it over his heart.

There, through the lamp-lit window, he could see his wife seated by the hearth, holding a large, fawn-colored bunny in her lap.

He ducked quickly through the low doorway and was glad to spy his hot supper on the table. But it was the warmth in Lydia's voice that made him feel happiest.

"Ah, John Sweeney!" she cried softly.

Laying the handmade bunny on the hearth, she flew to her young husband and kissed his rough cheek. "Your kidney pie has been calling you these last minutes!"

"I heard it from the lane."

"Sit down, then, and I'll fetch your tea. But first, do look at the bunny!"

John gave a gasp of approval as she held her creation before him.

"Ah, you're a clever lass, you are! He looks as true as any rabbit I've ever seen, with those brown eyes and all."

"Do you like him?" she asked, excited and pleased.

"More than a little, I do. He's the best, by far."

John bent down to admire his wife's handiwork more closely, and the delicacy of her stitches in the little blue jacket.

"Those silver buttons on his vest . . . now, where have I seen those buttons before, I wonder?" he asked.

Lydia blushed. "They're off your old coat. The one you've not worn, you said, since you were a lad."

"You're a robber and a thief!" cried John, as Lydia shrieked and ran to the singing teakettle.

In the kitchen, he caught her around the waist, laughing.

"Ah, Lydia. You can have my buttons, for you've already stolen my heart."

❖　　❖　　❖

The next morning, Lydia sat by the hearth with the bunny in her lap, and a sash of printed cotton.

"Now," she said, winding the little sash about his neck, "this will make you a completely finished rabbit, and when my wonderful bunny rabbits are completely finished, that's when I give them a name."

She looped the cotton tie quite carefully, so that the bow was crisp and neat.

"There! That's just *lovely*," she said, standing him up in her lap. "Now, let's give you a name!"

Lydia's eyes grew very bright as she pronounced his name: "Jeremy!"

She waited a moment.

"Now that you have a name, you may talk, you know."

Jeremy said nothing, because he had no idea what to say.

"My bunnies *always* talk when they're given their name," Lydia said patiently.

No sound but the crackling of the small fire on the hearth.

She looked into his brown eyes and grew worried. A little furrow appeared on her forehead.

Suddenly, Jeremy knew exactly what he wanted to say.

"Thank you!" he squeaked.

Lydia hugged him so hard he could scarcely breathe.

"I knew you'd talk!" she exclaimed. "I just knew it! But why are you thanking me?"

"For making me your very best bunny ever."

"Do you know what *else* I did, Jeremy?"

"Umm, no," he said.

"I also made you an honest bunny. That means that no matter what happens, you will always be honest, for that's the way you're made."

Lydia stood him upright in her lap, and a serious expression stole over her soft features.

"And speaking of honesty," she said, "someone has paid honest pounds sterling for you, and I've given them my honest word that I would send you off today."

"Do you send all your bunnies off?" Jeremy asked.

Lydia sighed. "Oh, yes. And it's harder and harder to do each time."

Lydia set him on the hearth, still warm from the early morning fire, and moved about the room picking up John's shirt and suspenders and tidying the table where they'd had morning tea.

There was quite a clatter of teacups and biscuit plates as Jeremy stood thinking over all she'd said.

"Where shall I be sent off *to*, exactly?"

He noticed that Lydia's chin quivered ever so slightly.

"America!" she said. "Where the cowboys are!"

"America!" exclaimed Jeremy. This news caused him to hop off the hearth and onto the worn rug. Perhaps he should hop under the table and hide, he thought.

Instead, he found that his legs liked so much to move that . . . they wouldn't stop!

He hopped around the old wooden floor, then raced into the kitchen and thumped the pine boards until it sounded like the drumming of a drum corps.

"Oh, Jeremy!" cried Lydia, clapping her hands with relief, "I just knew you'd be excited!"

Jeremy hopped across the room to Lydia's feet and looked up at her.

"I'm doing this because it feels good," he explained. "I'm not at all excited about going to America."

He saw that little furrow appear again on her brow.

"But I'll go," he said respectfully, and drummed his last upon the old cottage floor.

The Journey Begins

"We must hurry!" Lydia said, breathlessly. "The post will leave in less than an hour!

"I've addressed the box in a very large hand, so it can be easily read. And I've marked it **Fragile**."

Jeremy peered into the box which Lydia had taken from the cupboard. It was dark in that box. It was small in that box. It was lonely in that box.

Jeremy's eyes grew wider.

His ears stood straight up. Then he spoke with the same squeak he'd used to say his first words.

"I shall have to get to America some other way," he said, not wishing to be impertinent.

"Why, what do you mean?" asked Lydia.

His nose quivered, but only a bit. "I can't get in that box," he said.

"But it's a lovely box!" She fluffed the tissue paper, as if making an inviting nest. "You shall travel *ever* so smoothly in it!"

"If you don't mind," Jeremy said, weighing his words, "I'd rather make the journey on my own."

He felt very contrite, indeed, before the gentle Lydia.

"But how can you do that? You're only a . . . *home-made bunny!*"

"Yes, but I'm the best homemade bunny of all! You said so yourself!"

"However will you cross the ocean?"

Jeremy thought about this.

He looked down at his plaid trousers. He wiggled his nose. He closed his eyes and pondered.

Then he said, "I don't know. But I'll think of something!"

"I'm sure you will," said Lydia, growing convinced. "Goodness, I never dreamed I'd made such a determined bunny!"

She wrote something on a small slip of paper.

"You must keep this with you at all times," she said, tucking the slip of paper into his vest. "It's the name and address of the person you were made for, and you must deliver yourself as quickly as possible!"

He looked around the room, where Lydia had often sung lullabies as she sat with him in her lap, stitching his vest, sewing on the shiny buttons, and even creating his whiskers. Oh, this had been a lovely home! Perhaps he could somehow stay here, playing in the garden just beyond the door. . . .

But no, he was an honest bunny. And he had someone to deliver himself to.

"I believe in you," she said proudly, "for I know the way you're made."

Jeremy hopped to the open door and looked into the fragrant garden. A butterfly settled on a delphinium. A bee thrust itself into the blossom of a larkspur. Across the meadow, a lamb called.

Lydia knelt beside him and said:

"I have spoken to *my* maker about your journey, and you must carry these words with you:

"*For He shall give His angels charge over thee, to keep thee in all thy ways.*

"*They shall bear thee up in their hands, lest thou dash thy foot against a stone.*"

Jeremy nodded his head as Lydia bent down and straightened his tie.

Then he hopped through the open front door and bounded away, trying very hard to avoid looking back.

"Don't take carrots from strangers!" Lydia called as he hopped past the petunia bed.

"Keep your boots clean!

"Remember to polish your buttons!"

Now he was well into the lane, and his legs felt wonderfully swift and free.

A chipmunk dashed across his path.

A dove flew out of the hedge, its wings thrumming.

"Do keep your tie straight!" Lydia called.

Jeremy ran and ran and ran, not looking back. Then, when he reached the big woods, he stopped and turned around.

All he could see was a spiral of gray smoke rising from the cottage chimney.

A Stop Along the Way

$\mathcal{M}$r. Pruneholt was on his knees by the garden fence, weeding a bed of lupine and dusty miller.

"Out you come!" he said sternly, speaking to a dandelion which had made itself comfortable in the damp, sweet soil.

As he looked up to toss it in the basket, he spied a pair of large brown eyes staring brightly through the fence.

"Hullo!" Mr. Pruneholt exclaimed in surprise, dropping his trusty spade.

"Hello!" said Jeremy. "I'm looking for something special."

"Well, so am I," the old gardener said. "Always have been. That's just the way I am."

"I don't have much time," said Jeremy.

Mr. Pruneholt peered at Jeremy over his spectacles. "Who *does* these days?"

"I'm looking for America," confided the brown-eyed visitor. "Perhaps you can help me."

"I need help myself," Mr. Pruneholt said testily. "Help with digging the bulbs, help with spraying the roses, help with turning my compost . . ."

"I'll just be going on," said Jeremy, backing away.

Mr. Pruneholt scowled. "You're like everybody else

in these modern times, running off before you know where you're going!"

Jeremy thought the cranky Mr. Pruneholt needed a nap.

"Good-bye, then!" said Jeremy.

"Good-bye? Don't good-bye me, young fellow, you come inside and have some tea. I need someone to talk to. Cook is older than I am, if that's possible, and hardly ever passes a kind word."

"Oh, but I couldn't. . . ." said Jeremy.

"It's going to be a splendid tea, my boy. You won't find one like it again. No excuses, now, hop in here and bring your appetite." He swung the gate open for his reluctant guest. "We'll have cake and tea and feel like new, then I'll show you just where to head out!"

The old man rose stiffly to his feet and took a cane that was propped against a red barrow, and together they went up the flagstone walk to Mr. Pruneholt's crooked house under the trees.

A faint breeze ruffled the curtains in the dining room, where the table was set with cakes and short-bread, a pitcher of cream, cubes of sugar, pots of preserves, and other good things.

Pictures hung lopsided on the walls in the otherwise tidy room. And the wide, dark floorboards were dappled with a flood of afternoon light that entered the tall windows.

Jeremy sat in a Chippendale chair next to Mr. Pruneholt, who had forgotten to remove his cap.

The old gardener looked his guest in the eye. "To tell the truth," he said, "I never much liked rabbits."

"Really?" squeaked his guest.

"But you look a decent sort, tie and all that. Now, see here, these hearts are shortbread, made like my old nanny gave us for nursery tea. Cook just took them from the oven.

"And this . . ."

Suddenly, Mr. Pruneholt stopped in utter dismay.

"I *say!* I suppose you'll be wanting carrots and such!"

"Oh no," Jeremy said, helpfully. "Anything will do."

Mr. Pruneholt was vastly relieved and continued to point out the particulars of this very particular tea.

"Here's the cream, help yourself. Neighbor's cow. And this . . . oh, dear boy, *this* is my delight! Cook's specialty and my sworn favorite! English Rabbit!"

Jeremy's brown eyes grew as large as the saucers in a nursery teaset. His ears stood up quite straight.

"Good *heavens!*" said Mr. Pruneholt. "Now see what I've done. I've alarmed my guest! You *do* understand there's no *rabbit*, actually, in this Rabbit? Indeed *not,* my lad!"

He passed the piping hot plate quite close to his guest's nose, demonstrating by the delicious aroma that, indeed, there was no *actual* rabbit, English or otherwise, in this luscious dish.

Jeremy's nose twickered and twitched with anticipation.

"Thing about Rabbit, my boy, is that one must polish it off while the cheese is still hot. Now, *set to,*" said the old man, tucking a great square of damask under his chin.

Jeremy did as he was told. And found Mr. Pruneholt's English Rabbit quite the thing for a hungry bunny at teatime.

During their repast, Mr. Pruneholt poured Jeremy two cups of strong china tea, all the while talking as if he hadn't seen a soul for months, which he hadn't, really.

23

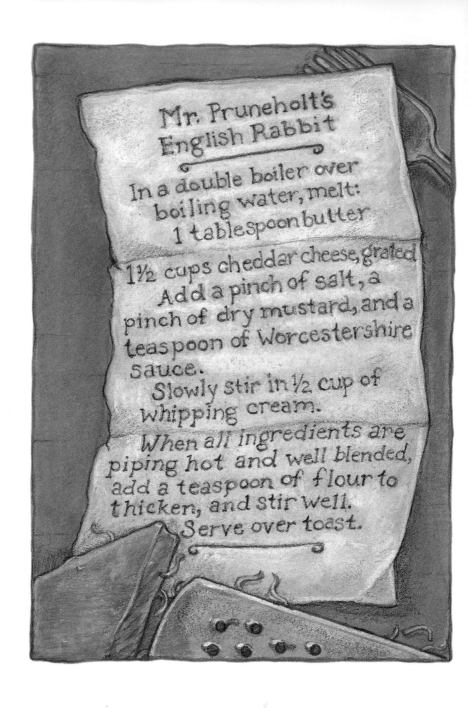

Mr. Pruneholt's English Rabbit

In a double boiler over boiling water, melt:
1 tablespoon butter

1½ cups cheddar cheese, grated
Add a pinch of salt, a pinch of dry mustard, and a teaspoon of Worcestershire sauce.
Slowly stir in ½ cup of whipping cream.

When all ingredients are piping hot and well blended, add a teaspoon of flour to thicken, and stir well.
Serve over toast.

Jeremy felt full as a tick, and his eyelids drooped heavily. In truth, he thought about having a nap. However, he had things to do and places to be.

"Well, sir, I must be off to America, for I'm delivering myself to someone, and I'm promised to arrive as soon as possible—ASAP is how it's put, I think."

"I don't suppose," said the old gardener, "that I could talk you into sticking around? You'd make a splendid hand in the garden, even if you are a rabbit."

Jeremy folded his napkin and excused himself respectfully from the table. "I don't believe so, sir."

Mr. Pruneholt sighed. "Oh, well. Never hurts to ask. Come along, then."

Down a dark hall they went and up the stairs and into a small, cozy library.

In the corner, next to an old leather wing chair, stood a great, round, glowing thing. Jeremy was transfixed by it.

"My world globe, lad, and a handsomer one you'll never see. I had the electric installed, so I could light it up! It's as fine a companion as the fire in the grate, and a deal more instructive. Now let's see . . ."

Mr. Pruneholt adjusted his glasses.

"Ah, here we are! If you go just *there* . . ." He pointed with his crooked finger, "That's where you'll find boats sailing to America!"

"But how do I *get* just there?" asked Jeremy.

"Why it's as simple as . . . as stirrin' your tea, actually. Just hop out of the gate, turn left by my rose bed, pass the mustard field on the right, our old church on the left, and keep straight till you smell salt air."

Jeremy patted the piece of paper inside his vest. He straightened his tie. Then he thanked Mr. Pruneholt for his help.

The old man suddenly smiled, his eyes twinkling. "I never liked rabbits, but you've been jolly good company. Call back if you pass this way again!"

Racing out the gate, Jeremy made a dash for the rose bed, which he recognized with his nose. Then he settled into a lope toward the mustard field.

Already his anticipation was rising for the smell of salt air, and for the someone he'd soon deliver himself to.

A Narrow Escape

$\mathcal{I}$t wasn't long before Jeremy found himself in a large park with benches and a splashing fountain.

Nannies and nursemaids were gathered around the fountain, talking to one another and jiggling the prams of their charges.

Jeremy, who was nibbling on a clump of tasty dandelions, looked up and saw two small people running across the lawn toward a nanny in a white hat.

One small person had long golden hair and wore a frock with a pinafore.

The other small person had short golden hair and wore a jacket and trousers.

Otherwise, they looked just alike.

Suddenly, he realized they were running toward *him*.

"Wook! A *wabbit!*" they shouted.

"A *wittle* wabbit!" they squealed.

"Wet's get it!"

"Twins!" called their nanny. "Come back here *at once!*"

But the twins, for all their fat, short legs and stout little frames, were as fleet as the wind, and quickly raced out of earshot of the earnest young woman.

Jeremy saw the nanny bolt off the bench in pursuit of the twins, holding on to her hat.

"Twins! Come back *now,* or you shall *never* have a bite of cake *again!"*

Jeremy stared wide-eyed at the two small people tearing straight for him, and knew one thing for certain:

He must run for his life!

"Wook at his wittle cwothes!"

"He wearin' wittle booties, too!"

"I catch him first!"

"I catch him first!"

If Jeremy had been a cat, he could have climbed a tree. If he'd been a dog, he could have barked savagely. But Jeremy was a rabbit. So, he did what rabbits do. He scurried under a fence, and not a moment too soon.

"Wook!" cried the twins. "De wabbit is wunnin' to de big fwimmin' pool!"

"To de *boats!"*

"Wet's go wif 'im!"

The twin in the little jacket rolled under the fence, slick as you please.

The nanny came running over the hill, shouting, "Not a *bite,* do you hear, not for a *hundred years!"*

The twin in the pinafore also scrambled under the fence. "You big dummy wabbit!" she wailed. "Don't wun so fast, I goin' to hold you!"

The nanny leaped the fence, skirts flying, and joined

the little procession of rabbit and twins streaking toward the water.

"You'll never get sugar in your tea again, never! Never, never, ever!" The nanny's hat sailed off her head and landed in a bush.

Suddenly, Jeremy heard a great thump and turned to see the twin in the pinafore go sprawling to the ground. Then the twin in the little jacket tumbled over the twin in the pinafore and crashed to the grass, shrieking.

Jeremy covered his eyes as the nanny tripped over them both, and down the hill they rolled.

Panting, he veered toward the great regiment of boats, looking over his shoulder all the while. He needed to find the rest of the way to America, fast, while there was still something left to deliver.

Crash!

Jeremy ran into something very, very large. He was knocked to the ground.

He looked up to see a man in a fine blue coat and trousers peering down at him. He had bushy, wild eyebrows, but his face was gentle.

"You'd better watch where you're goin', young fella!"

"I'm going to America," said Jeremy. He stood up and brushed off his soiled jacket. Lydia wouldn't like this.

"Well, so are we, so are we! How're you sailin'?"

"Any way I can," said Jeremy.

The man roared with laughter. "Come with me, then. Off we go."

A hand as large as a dinner plate came down and scooped Jeremy up, up, up, until he looked into a pair of shining blue eyes.

"I always liked rabbits," said the captain.

Over the Bounding Sea

Jeremy had never seen the ocean; he had never seen a wave; he had never seen a gull. And he had certainly never seen two great, silver moons at the same time— one in the sky and one in the water.

Jeremy was put into the captain's cabin and given a lovely wooden crate to sleep in. He was also given a soft blanket, two small pillows, and all the carrots he could eat. He wasn't allowed on deck, however, without the captain.

"You must watch yourself, my boy, or you'll end up in a stew, carrots and all!"

The captain threw back his head and laughed a big laugh.

"Ha, ha," said Jeremy.

He shared the cabin with the captain's parrot whose name was Jethro. Jethro could imitate almost anything: steamship whistles, foghorns, a crowd cheering at a parade, jets flying in formation, air escaping from a tire. He liked to make these sounds throughout the day, with hardly any letup at all.

Jeremy tried and tried to nap, for the rocking of the boat made him very sleepy.

"Please, please, *please* be quiet," he said to the bird with the colorful feathers.

"Quiet? All these years learning to talk, to do these great impressions, and you ask me to be quiet? Have you heard my windshield wiper?"

Jeremy put a pillow over his head and covered his ears.

"Shhh-tick, shhh-tick, shhh-tick, shhh-tick . . ." said Jethro. "What do you think?"

Jeremy put the other pillow over his head.

Day after day, the boat rode the waves toward America.

Jeremy found there was hardly anything to do but eat and sleep, sleep and eat. Jethro, however, was finding all sorts of things to do. Currently, he was imitating the sound of a bow scraped across the strings of a sailor's fiddle.

Scrape, scrape, scrape, scrape.

Jeremy had never heard such an awful sound in his life. If he could have gotten the porthole open, he would have jumped into the water—and he didn't even know how to swim!

One morning, after scraps of cabbage leaves and radish tops, Jeremy had an idea.

"Jethro, can you make your fiddle play music?"

"Music? You want *music?"*

"Well, I mean, yes, if you don't mind."

"Music," muttered Jethro, scratching his head with his wing. "You give 'em parades, you give 'em jets in formation—and what do they want? *Music!*"

Jeremy sighed.

Jethro flew out of his open cage and landed on the captain's table. He marched around for a moment, as if thinking. Then he threw his head back and opened his beak.

First, Jeremy heard the lilting music of a flute.

Then, the rich, melodious notes of an oboe.

Next, he heard a French horn followed by kettle drums, a bassoon, and a tuba!

"What do you think?" asked Jethro, pleased with himself.

"Great!" said Jeremy. "But I was wondering—could you maybe . . . sing a lullaby?" He remembered Lydia's lullabies, which she often sang as she sat by the hearth.

Jethro looked disgusted. "I don't do lullabies. No harpsichords, upright spinets, or lullabies. Geez, I wish I had an agent."

"Um, could you sing a cowboy song?"

Jethro flapped his wings and flew to the captain's chair, and perched on the back. He looked at the ceiling. He wiggled his foot. "Got it!" he shouted.

"Got what?" asked Jeremy.

"Okay, okay, here we go," said Jethro. "You're gonna love this. Ready? Listen up!"

As the boat sailed over the bounding sea, Jethro squawked at the top of his lungs, *"I'm an ol' cowhand, from th' Rio Grande . . ."*

Jeremy's eyes closed very slowly.

Then his head dropped.

Next, his ears flopped.

"But my legs ain't bowed and my cheeks ain't tanned . . ."

Jeremy didn't hear another word of the cowboy song, for he was fast asleep on his pillow.

Safely Across

*O*h, he was glad to be on solid ground again!

Just this morning, his boat had sailed into a big port, the hull hitting the dock. *Bump! Thunk!*

Jeremy had lost his balance and gone skidding along the slippery deck. *Whoosh!*

Gulls had flown overhead, screeching. Deckhands shouted and scurried about. And waves lapped the ship's hull as the gangplank came down. *Blam!*

"There you are, young fellow!" The captain scooped

Jeremy into his hand, and set him on his broad shoulders. Then he strode down the gangplank with the parrot cage, shouting, "Barbecue and fried chicken, here I come! No more dried kippers, I'm kippered out!"

"He's kippered out!" squawked Jethro.

Away from the great bustle and clamor of the dock, the captain stopped and set the parrot cage down. Then he placed Jeremy in the grass and squatted beside him.

"Well, lad, off with you now. Head in the direction I told you, and in no time at all, you'll find yourself delivered. I must deliver myself to someone, as well. My good wife and children haven't laid eyes on me in a month of Sundays!"

Jeremy thanked the captain, said good-bye to Jethro, and raced away at once, not looking back.

"So, long, Big Ears!" yelled Jethro.

Now, here he was in America, tucked safely into the hollow of an oak tree and shielded from the late summer rain. His wet jacket hung on a twig inside the tree's opening and dripped onto a floor of earth as soft as a worn Aubusson carpet.

He peered into the countryside, searching for a cowboy. Ah, well! Pehaps cowboys didn't come out in the rain.

He turned his attention instead to his dry, cozy quarters. "This would do nicely for a cottage!" he said aloud. "Why, there's already a coat hook and a soft floor for long naps!"

"Don't get too comfortable, buster," said a booming voice.

Jeremy nearly jumped out of his boots.

"But where . . . ?"

"Up here," said the voice. "Would you kindly cut th'chatter, I've had a long night."

Jeremy trembled. *"Who . . . ?"*

"And don't go mocking me, you little squirt."

Two big, luminous eyes peered down from above.

"Are you a *cowboy?*" asked Jeremy.

"I'm Charles Benchley Owl, Chuck to my friends, and this tree is taken."

An owl! He'd heard owls hooting outside the little cottage many a night, and the sound had made him shiver even before Lydia gave him a name and he became real.

"Excuse me, sir, I've traveled a long way and I thought I might just take a nap, but I'll be m-m-moving right along. . . ."

"Don't worry! Good thing for you, I gave up rabbit years ago, gives me gas."

The owl burped, which in the great hollow sounded like a cannon's roar.

Jeremy snatched his jacket off the hook and was

ready to make tracks. "I certainly don't want to intrude. . . ."

"No big deal," said the owl. "Lie down and take a little snooze before you hit the road. Do you snore?"

"I don't know," said Jeremy.

"If you snored, you'd know it. You'd wake yourself up."

"I guess I don't snore, then."

"Good! Have a nap and make it snappy!"

Hardly any time passed before Jeremy heard an awful racket above his head. It was the owl, and he was snoring.

Before drifting off to sleep, Jeremy looked out through the misty curtain of gray rain to rolling hills, a tidy fence, a field of green corn, and cows huddling under a tree.

It looked just like England!

He wanted nothing more than to stay right here, in this snug, warm home. But . . .

He put his paw inside his vest.

There, warm from being carried next to his heart, was the piece of folded paper.

"Oh, my," said Jeremy. "I already *have* a home! And I must get there *soon!*"

He held the paper up to the light and, written in Lydia's neat hand, he read:

You were made for:
Candace Freeland
(here followed an address)
North Carolina
U.S.A.
Please hurry, Jeremy!
Love, Lydia

How could he have forgotten?

He was going where there was someone to love him, and someone for him to love back!

Would she have a cat? He hoped not!

Would she have a garden? He hoped so!

Would she drink tea and tell him stories? And would she have fair hair, or be dark-haired like Lydia?

"Her name is free land," Jeremy thought proudly. "I like that!"

The Village Dear

After his nap, and a sincere thank you to Charles Benchley Owl, Jeremy left the snug tree behind.

The rain had stopped, and a glorious day spread before him.

Somewhere in a meadow, he heard a sheep. *Baa-aa-aa-a!*

Somewhere in a tree, he heard a squirrel. *Cuckcuckcuck.*

Somewhere in the clean air, he smelled fresh-mown hay.

His nose never stopped twitching, his feet never stopped hopping. Until he came to the garden.

He peeked through the open gate and looked around curiously.

A peach tree cast its shade upon the path. . . .

An old, old, apple tree grew near a garden bench. . . .

A carpet of mown grass, glistening and perfect as a bolt of velvet, was unfurled on the garden floor.

Near it was a chair with someone in it, someone who was fast, fast asleep. As Jeremy stood looking on, a book slipped out of the sleeping someone's hand and fell open in the grass.

Eagerly, Jeremy hopped into the garden and paused in a shaft of late morning light.

"Oh, my," said a small, rather old woman with lots of curls about her face. "I must have nodded off!"

She was wearing a pair of stockings rolled below her

knees and needlepoint slippers dusted with flour from a pie she had baked this morning.

"Excuse me, please," said Jeremy. "Is this North Carolina?"

"Indeed not!" replied the small woman, indignant. "It's Virginia!"

She leaned forward in her chair to peer down at him. "My, you're tall for your age," she said. "But, nonetheless, blue is certainly your most flattering color.

"Do you know there have been moles here all morning? They've burrowed under my chair the live-long day, and not one has come forward with so much as a 'Thank you, ma'am.'"

In a huff, she moved from her chair to the bench. "Moles are everlastingly ill-bred, and believe me, Mr. Piggs is furious about it!"

She had little round smudges of rouge on her cheeks and skin that appeared as fresh as a girl's. "But let's not dwell on dark thoughts!" she said.

"No ma'am!" agreed Jeremy.

"Come sit beside me and we'll take a nice drive in the country!"

She patted the bench and beckoned to her visitor, who popped up beside her.

"You *would* like a nice drive in my carriage?"

Jeremy thought about this. "But we . . . don't have a horse."

"Fiddle dee dee, indeed we do. Steady, now, Natasha!" she said to the morning air, and took up the reins of her imaginary mare.

"Whoa, girl! There now, nice and easy, it's out of the gate and away we go!"

Suddenly, Jeremy thought his coattails might be flying. He thought his ears might be standing perpendicular to the carriage seat.

He heard the wind rushing by as she called out, "Over there is Captain Stuart's house, where we had fancy balls every spring! And over there . . . do you see over there?"

He thought he certainly did. "Yes, ma'am."

"That's where we picked apples by the river! And went on picnics every summer!"

Jeremy held onto the arm of the carriage for dear life, though the ride was so smooth as to be nearly motionless. Natasha must be picking up her feet very smartly.

"Oh, heavenly *days!*" whooped his happy driver. "These cool mornings make our little mare fly! Young man, you must give her an apple when we return home."

Just then, a kind-looking gentleman appeared alongside them.

"Mornin', ma'am. Out for your drive, are you?"

"Whoa, Natasha. Yes, Piggs. And we need apples right away!"

Mr. Piggs pulled three apples from his sweater pocket and handed one to his mistress and one to her guest. They all bit right in and began to chew contentedly.

"This lovely young gentleman is riding out with me this morning."

"We don't get many rabbits," said Mr. Piggs, peering at Jeremy on the garden bench. Jeremy somehow knew the ride was over, as his driver seemed to have forgotten all about it.

"Squirrels, now, we *do* get squirrels. . . ."

"And moles!" said his mistress.

"Oh, yes, indeed! Moles by the dozens!"

"Put Natasha in the barn, Piggs, and I'll pour up some lemonade."

The small woman with the flour on her shoes trotted along the path and disappeared into the large, white house.

"Who is that lady?" asked Jeremy.

"That's the village dear, she is."

"The village dear?"

"Yes, indeed. The people here love her, for she's kind and makes them happy. And so they call her the village dear, you see."

Mr. Piggs bit into his apple and chewed noisily.

"I've been gardenin' here since she was a little young'un, nearly seventy-five years. She likes her flowers and her fruit trees and all, and I like to keep 'em for her, and so we get along just right, we do."

"Could you tell me how to find North Carolina?" Jeremy inquired.

"Why, sure, young fella. But first, I got to put this mare in the barn, or she'll give me what for, she will."

Mr. Piggs led Natasha out of the garden and through the gate, not caring at all that she was invisible.

Jeremy looked down at the book that lay open on the grass, and his gaze fell upon these words:

For He shall give His angels charge over thee, to keep thee in all thy ways.
They shall bear thee up in their hands, lest thou dash thy foot against a stone.

That was what Lydia had written on the paper he carried over his heart!

There were lots of other words on the page, which was marked *Psalm 91*, but before he could read them, Village Dear returned with a tray containing a pitcher of lemonade and three small glasses.

"Where are you off to, young man? You're mighty dandied up!"

"I'm off to my new home in North Carolina."

"I couldn't bear to live anyplace but Virginia," she said wistfully, forgetting to pour the lemonade. "It's where I met Captain Stuart, you see."

"I'm going to like North Carolina," he said. "I'm going to belong to Candace!"

"Did you say 'candance'?"

"I don't know if she can dance," said Jeremy, who secretly hoped she could.

"I can dance," said Village Dear, who proceeded to stand on her tiptoes and twirl around twice before she crashed onto the cushion in her chair.

"Oopsy daisy!" she exclaimed.

Mr. Piggs came up the path, holding his hat in both hands.

"Looky what I've got here!" he said.

Village Dear peered into his hat, and gasped. Then she giggled. "Bunnies!"

Jeremy leaned over as far as he could, to see for himself.

"Just awhile ago," Mr. Piggs remarked, "I said we don't get many rabbits . . . and now . . ."

"When it rains, it pours," exclaimed Village Dear.

There they were, two little ones with long ears, asleep, and lying so close to one another they might have been one bunny with two tails.

"Found 'em in a stump behind th' shed. Ol' Harry was barkin' and yappin' so, I was afraid to leave 'em."

Jeremy looked at the bunnies in astonishment. He was glad he'd never looked like *that!* Why, they had no vests with silver buttons, no jackets, no boots, nothing!

"Where's their mother?" asked Village Dear.

"Ol' Harry's run their mama off, is what I'd say. Dogs are mighty scornful of rabbits, you know." Mr. Piggs turned to Jeremy. "What do you think we should do, young fella?"

Never in all his life had anyone asked him what to do about anything.

Jeremy closed his eyes and thought very, very hard.

In his mind, he saw the old oak tree standing in the meadow in the sunshine.

"I know a perfect place for their home," he said happily. "There aren't any dogs around, just squirrels and . . ." He didn't think he should mention the owl, no indeed. He didn't know how, but he would work it out with the owl, one way or another, even if he had to pay rent by giving over . . . what? His silver buttons.

"You come in handy," said Village Dear, and proceeded to drop off to sleep in her chair.

Mr. Piggs picked up the book and gently laid it on the bench.

"Let's go along," he said to Jeremy. "We'll take these little 'uns to your place and get 'em settled in."

Setting Up Housekeeping

$\mathcal{M}$r. Piggs thought it best to leave the bunnies asleep in his hat, and so he very tenderly placed it in the farthest curve of the tree's warm, dark hollow.

"Oh, my," said Jeremy. "That's too fine a hat to leave in a tree. I can make them a lovely bed with my jacket."

"Well, now, that's a good thought. But you see, they've had enough change for awhile, and they've snuggled right in like it was home."

Home! Jeremy liked that word.

"When they're up and out on their own," said the

old man, "I'll come and fetch my hat, and a sight better it'll be for the wear."

"I can't stay long," said Jeremy, "but I'll see to their first night or so, and help them find their tea in the morning."

"That's a good lad. Well, I'll just be goin' along, now. But to tell the truth," Mr. Piggs patted his gray head, "I feel part of me is missin'."

Jeremy looked up at the kindly man with the wrinkled face.

"Ah, excuse me, sir. Which way is North Carolina?"

Mr. Piggs thought hard.

He stood on one foot. Then he stood on the other.

He scratched his head. He cleared his throat. And then he pointed.

"That way," he said firmly, and set off through the meadow, looking back twice to wave.

Right away, Jeremy made himself busy.

He dug up small tufts of moss and stuffed them in his jacket pocket to line the floor of the tree hollow.

He had put down only three fine tufts, when two bright eyes peered over the old hat brim.

"Hello!" said Jeremy.

"Hello, yourself!" said a wee voice.

"What's your name?" asked Jeremy.

"Hazel," said the baby rabbit.

The other baby rabbit popped up beside Hazel. "And I'm Percy!"

"Who are *you?*" they wanted to know.

"Jeremy."

"Is that a *name?*" Hazel wondered.

"Indeed it is. How do you like your new home?"

Four bright eyes looked around the cozy hollow.

"Are there any dogs here?"

"No dogs," promised Jeremy.

"Are there any owls here?"

"Ah . . . well . . . " said Jeremy. He'd quite forgotten

about Benchley Whatever-his-name-was! He peered up into the tree, anxiously. "Are you home, Mr. Benchley?"

He didn't dare say "Chuck."

But there was no answer.

All afternoon, the bunnies played near the tree, finding delicious nibbles in the grass and sweet heads of clover.

"Yum, yum, yum, *yum!*" squealed Hazel, while Jeremy finished laying his thick moss carpet.

The owl, thought Jeremy, would be happy to rent his tree in exhange for the buttons. Besides, he would pull the thread out of his vest so neatly that no one could guess buttons had ever been there. He knew Lydia would not mind him doing this—after all, it was for the bunnies.

As dusk came, the bunnies were weary from play and enormously satisfied with their scrumptious feast of forget-me-nots, clover, bluets, and buttercups. They popped back into their hat, and Jeremy told them a story about his trip across the great water, how he had lived in the captain's quarters and was treated to all the finest scraps, including melon rinds and cabbage. The little crate that had been his home had rocked like a cradle as the boat sailed the foaming waves.

The very moment Jeremy finished his tale, Hazel peered over the hat brim.

"I want my mama!" she said. A big tear rolled into her whiskers.

Up bobbed Percy, his nose quivering. "I want my mama!"

"We want our mama!" they cried together.

"Oh *dear!*" said Jeremy, who began rocking the hat.

"We want our mama!" They cried even louder and Jeremy rocked even harder.

"What'n the dickens is goin' on down there?" came a booming voice.

The crying stopped at once. The hair stood up on Jeremy's neck.

"We're just settling in," Jeremy squeaked.

"Settlin' in? Is that th' jackleg rabbit who holed up down there this afternoon?"

"One and the same," Jeremy said, still squeaking.

"Dadgummit, what does a critter have to do to get some rest in 'is own tree? And who's that doin' all th' bawlin'?"

"It's me, Hazel!" said Hazel, sniffling.

"And me, Percy!" said Percy, also sniffling.

Jeremy screwed up his courage. "Their mother is indisposed for a time, and they need a home."

"Everybody needs a home," said the owl, grumpily.

"This is the perfect home for Hazel and Percy, and I'll pay you to let them stay here."

"Pay me with what?"

"Buttons!"

"Buttons? You're kidding me."

"Seriously," said Jeremy. "Could you look down here a moment?"

He would just take off his vest and hold it as high as he could, so the owl could see the fine silver buttons. . . .

Suddenly the owl flew down into the hollow, his great wings flapping. The bunnies shrieked with horror. Jeremy felt every hair on his body stand bolt upright.

"Oh, *hush*," said the owl to the bunnies. "I'm harm-

less. I haven't eaten a bunny in ages, and don't intend to. I've developed rather a taste for—"

"Shhh," said Jeremy. "Don't say that sort of thing in front of—"

"Hershey Bars," finished the owl.

Jeremy and the bunnies sighed with relief.

"I like your big *wings*," said Hazel.

"I like your *legs*," said Percy. "Fluffy!"

"Why, thanks," said Chuck, looking pleased.

By the time Jeremy awoke, the sun had climbed above the trees.

Chuck had told bedtime stories until the wee hours, and everyone had giggled and laughed till they fell asleep, which was very late indeed. In fact, Chuck had invited them all to stay in the tree as long as they cared to, since he only used the top limbs, anyway.

Leaving the bunnies still sleeping, Jeremy crept out to the dew-kissed meadow.

Oh, but it was a dazzling day! A day that would be perfect for going to North Carolina.

But if he left the bunnies now, there was no telling what might happen. If they started missing their mother again, they could drown in their own tears. And he didn't think Chuck was exactly the fatherly type. . . .

He knew he couldn't go to Candace today.

Yet, what would Lydia think of him for such a long delay? She had, after all, made him to be an *honest* bunny, and she *had* asked him to hurry.

While he thought deeply on this troubling matter, something stirred in the grass.

He sat quite still.

Only his whiskers twitched.

Homeward Bound

*S*uddenly a small brown rabbit dashed from the tall grass and boldly hopped up to him.

"S-s-sir," quaked the brown rabbit, "I demand that you hand over my bunnies this v-v-v-very *instant*."

Jeremy was startled, to say the least. Before him stood a beautiful rabbit with soft, amber eyes, a fringe of dark lashes, and the tiniest powdering of white on her paws.

Obviously it had taken great courage for the rabbit to confront Jeremy, for she was trembling with fear even as she stood before him.

"You m-m-must hand them over *now*, s-sir!"

"Who are you?" he asked, noticing that this rabbit

looked just like Hazel and Percy, except she was a bit taller.

"Their m-m-*mother,* sir!"

"Mama!" Jeremy heard Hazel squeal.

"Mama!" called Percy.

In a flash, the green grass was alive with joyous bunnies rolling and tumbling, nipping and leaping, and Jeremy couldn't tell where one ended and the other two began.

When the fuss died down and the children had taken off after a butterfly, Jeremy said, "I didn't steal Hazel and Percy, for I am an honest bunny. I brought them here so they'd be safe."

"Then thank you very *much.* I should have known, for you have an honest face, sir."

Jeremy looked at the toes of his boots. "You don't have to call me sir."

"But you *look* like a sir in your lovely jacket," she said.

"It's my travel jacket. I'm on my way to North Carolina, to deliver myself to Candace."

"Oh!" sighed the brown rabbit, quite dazzled.

"And now that you've come, I must be moving on."

"I wish . . . you would stay," the brown rabbit said, without any of the little stammer she'd had when she was afraid of him.

Jeremy looked at Hazel and Percy flying around the edge of the meadow, leaping over the clover patches.

He looked at the great green swell of the hills beyond, and up into the protective branches of the oak.

What a fine home it was! And what a splendid neighborhood!

"I must go," he said at last. "But come and see the home we've found, I'm sure you can stay here as long as you like."

Jeremy showed her around the cool, dark interior of the old tree trunk. She exclaimed with delight over the green carpet, and the brown hat that Mr. Piggs had broken in until it was nearly as soft as Hazel's ears.

"Why, this is the loveliest home I've ever seen!"

"There aren't any dogs around, and you and the bunnies will be safe here. But there's something I should tell you."

The brown rabbit looked at him with large, soft eyes.

"Chuck lives upstairs!"

"Who's Chuck?"

There was a great thrumming of wings, as the owl swooped down onto the moss carpet.

"That would be me," said Chuck, who bowed slightly.

Jeremy held on to the horrified brown rabbit, who was trying to escape. "He's okay, I promise! Don't run! He doesn't eat bunnies!"

"Gives me gas," said Chuck. "You th' mama?"

"Y-y-y-yes, sir."

"Fine kids you got there. Y'all make yourselves at home, stay as long as you like, I come and go mostly durin' th' night, but I'll try to keep the racket down. Want a bite of my Hershey? They say it's not good for your teeth, but since I don't have any, what th' hey!"

Jeremy couldn't put it off a moment longer. He had to be on his way.

He stood on one hind foot and then the other. "Mr. Piggs," he told the brown rabbit, "may come and get his hat when Hazel and Percy are grown."

"I don't know how to thank you," the brown rabbit said wistfully.

"No need to thank me," Jeremy told her. For some reason, he felt the silver buttons were going to pop off his vest.

"Is this good-bye then?"

Jeremy looked deep into her large, soft eyes, and felt he was falling down, down, down. . . .

But he could not tell a lie. "Yes. And I must be going before the sun gets higher!"

"Percy! Hazel! Come and say good-bye!" their mother called.

The bunnies raced to fling themselves on him, with Hazel

giving big, wet kisses and Percy trying to unlace his boots.

"Don't go!" cried Percy.

"Oh, stay!" implored Hazel. "We were just starting to have fun!"

"Oh, *dear!*" Jeremy sighed.

"Did you call me?" asked the brown rabbit, batting her long lashes.

But Jeremy patted the little ones on their heads and scampered away as fast as he could go.

He will send His angels before you, to keep you in all your ways. . . .

Jeremy wondered for the first time who He was. Just before he reached the fence, Jeremy stopped and looked back. Chuck was sitting on the lowest limb of the oak, telling funny stories. The bunnies were rolling in the grass, laughing.

As he hopped away, Jeremy tried to laugh, too. But he could not.

A Desperate Encounter

*F*or a long, long time, Jeremy went as straight in the direction of North Carolina as he could possibly go.

Every day he looked for cowboys, but he didn't find any.

Several times he was chased by angry, snarling dogs who had no hospitality at all toward strangers.

And once, when he reached the mountains, he saw a huge black bear with her cub, which forced him to detour through a ravine full of brambles.

One morning near the end of his journey, he

noticed with some alarm a tiny hole in his boot. His jacket was considerably frayed. And somehow, his lovely, patterned necktie was woefully limp.

He sighed as he hopped toward his final destination.

He came to a wide valley where cows grazed, and someone, far off, was hauling wood on a sled pulled by a horse with ruffles on its ankles.

He saw little brown bunnies racing across the fields and kept his eyes open for foxes that might be looking for him to pass. When he loped through a field of dried, rustling cornstalks, a congregation of crows started up, squawking.

This was certainly no place to try and mend his boot, he thought. But it was a lovely place to take a nap.

As he settled under a rhododendron bush at the foot of a hill, he noticed a sudden chill in the air. Then a light wind whipped up, and he buttoned all the buttons on his vest and pulled his jacket close around him.

Jeremy wished he could see one of those angels Lydia had talked about. Where were they? And what did an angel look like, anyway?

Jeremy felt very, very tired and scooted his back against the trunk of the rhododendron to keep the wind off. He dropped his head and closed his eyes. Just a little rest, just a little. . . .

Suddenly, there came a sound of snapping twigs and

rustling leaves. He opened his eyes and saw a red fox with its wicked, slobbering tongue hanging out. The fox was ready to lap Jeremy up and crush his neck between sharp and hideous teeth.

Jeremy bounded away as fast as he could go, his heart hammering in his ears as he searched frantically for a safe hole or burrow. But he was in a strange land and saw no refuge anywhere.

Then, all at once, a high rock wall loomed ahead, and Jeremy felt the scalding breath of the fox on his tail and hind legs.

Jeremy darted to the right.

The fox darted to the right.

Jeremy darted to the left.

The fox darted to the left.

There was no escape. With his heart nearly pounding out of his chest, Jeremy closed his eyes and turned to face his attacker.

The fox, baring razor-sharp teeth in a terrible grin, said: "Gotcha-a-a-a!"

The Snow Angel

"Begone, you!" shouted a thunderous voice. "Be off, you miserable wretch!"

Jeremy looked up to see a gaunt old man with a great mane of silver hair. He wore a rusty black suit and carried a black book in his hand.

The man raised the book and shouted again as the red fox bolted from sight with its tail between its legs.

Before Jeremy could dash away, the old man bent down and peered at him. Jeremy felt the man's bright, shining eyes pierce him straight through, and something in Jeremy's heart tingled.

"Young fellow, do you know where you're going?"

"Oh, y-yes, sir," replied Jeremy.

"Splendid!" said the old man, still bending down and still peering. "Then you know you've been purchased with a price!"

"Oh, yes sir, I do."

"And that you'll someday go to live in a heavenly home, with the One who has bought you?"

"Oh, yes, sir. In-d-d-deed," shivered Jeremy in the fresh, cold air.

The old man raised up stiffly. "Well, son, may He

give His angels charge over thee. . . ." A snowflake fell upon his black suit.

"To keep me in all my ways?" asked Jeremy, remembering what Lydia had said when she told him goodbye.

"Yes, my boy, in all your ways."

Many snowflakes were swirling down now. "Well, sir, thank you very much. I must be on my way."

"And not a moment too soon. They're calling for six inches tonight!"

He watched the old man stride toward the meadow, fit as a youth. As he reached the tractor path that ran through the meadow, he turned and waved. "Remember Preacher Greer!" he called out to Jeremy.

Jeremy didn't know what snow was, exactly, but he felt a need to hurry.

He also didn't know for absolutely, positively certain what an angel was. But he believed he'd just seen one.

And maybe . . . Jeremy stopped for a moment and thought. Maybe he had seen angels all along the way. . . .

Though he shivered in his thin jacket, his heart felt as warm as buttered toast for tea.

Just ahead, he saw a steep hill, something like a mountain.

With his last strength of the day, he trudged up, up, up, dodging brambles and twigs that snatched at his clothes. He climbed uphill for what seemed a very long time, until he came to a low stone wall where he stopped to rest.

Somehow, he sensed he was farther west than he meant to be. And oh, he felt he'd been delivering himself to Candace for such a very long time!

Slowly, he hopped down the road until he came to a small, pink house with a rose arbor and a picket fence. Snowflakes swirled around him, and he felt the cold through the little hole in his boot.

MAY ALL WHO ENTER HERE BE BLESSED, read a sign by the door. Jeremy felt encouraged at once. Perhaps he might rest here!

He knocked, and someone came to the door.

"I'm delivering myself to Candace," explained Jeremy, "and I think I'm lost."

"Lost? Indeed *not!*" said the someone, inviting him in. "Why, Candace is due to arrive any moment now! You may consider yourself *delivered!*"

He was led into a room with a crackling fire on the hearth, and somewhere he heard a teakettle singing. Then, just inside another door, in a room warmed by lamplight, he spied a large, inviting bed.

"Oh!" said Jeremy. With a little sigh, he scrambled onto the bed at once. "I think I need a bit of . . . a bit of . . ."

In less time than it takes for a snowflake to fall, Jeremy fell fast asleep on the pillow.

Which is just how Candace found him when she arrived for Christmas at Rosegate.